Published by Calithumpian Press, LLC
CalithumpianPress.com

Book designed by Paul Williams and edited by Lisa Pliscou.

The text in this book is "Neutra Text TF" by House Industries, and the font for the title is Elroy.

The PLAY-DOH® name and packaging are registered trademarks of Hasbro. Use of the product name and image does not imply any affiliation with or endorsement by Hasbro. But c'mon - we think it's pretty clever that KeeKee thinks *Plato* is *Play-Doh*, don't you? And who doesn't LOVE Play-Doh? We had the Fuzzy Pumper Barber Shop when we were young - so much fun!

First Edition – 2015

Library of Congress Control Number: 2014914553
Cataloging-In-Publication Data available

ISBN: 978-0-9886341-2-1

Printed in the United States of America
by Phoenix Color, Hagerstown, Maryland.

10 9 8 7 6 5 4 3 2 1 ... and away she goes!

KeeKeesBigAdventures.com
Facebook: KeeKee's Big Adventures
Twitter: @KeeKeeAdventure

CALITHUMPIAN
PRESS

To the inspirations for
KeeKee's Big Adventures...
Our kitties, KeeKee and Luna, and all the fabulous friends we've made on our travels, including
Cristina, Arne, Odilia, Melle, Marijn, Manolis, Ulla, Gulben & Peppe.

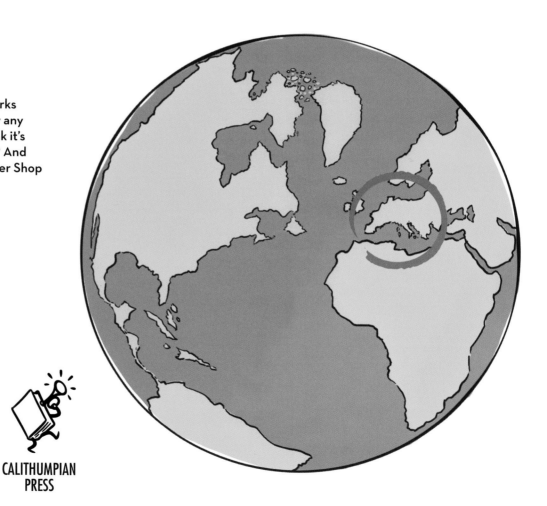

KeeKee's Big Adventures^{tm}
in Athens, Greece

Story by Shannon Jones

Illustrations by Casey Uhelski

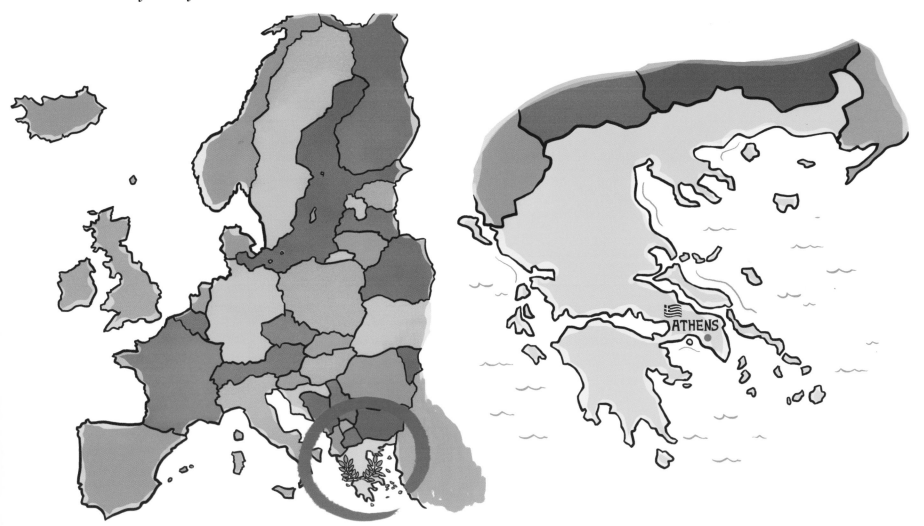

ATHENS

"*Yiá sas!* Hello!" said Manolis.
"*Kalós orísate!*
Welcome to one of the
oldest cities in the world!"

"Thank you! *Efcharistó!*" said KeeKee.
"Wow, there's the Parthenon!
Monument to the goddess Athena!"

"Yes, our city is named after her," Manolis said.
"And now we're working hard to put this
incredible building back together."

Manolis showed KeeKee
around the Parthenon,
telling her how it would have looked
thousands of years ago.

Amazing!

"I must get back to work," said Manolis.
"But I have a friend who is an Athens expert!"

"The world's first theater and plays began right here in Athens," said Evi.

"Look! It's the Greek gods!" said KeeKee.

I'm Zeus... ruler of the gods.

"Here we are in Plaka,"
Evi said. "It's the oldest
neighborhood in Athens, and
it *still* has wonderful shops,
restaurants, and *tavernas*."

Kaliméra!
Good
morning!

"It's all Greek to me," said KeeKee. "Let's eat!"

"Moussaká... and olives... and *tzatzíki*... oh my!" KeeKee chanted as they enjoyed the yummy Greek food.

chomp chomp

Kalí órexi.

Enjoy
your meal.

"Whoosh! I'm as stuffed
as an olive!" giggled KeeKee.

"Then it's the perfect time for
some exercise," said Evi.

"Greeks invented the Olympics," said Evi. "Games have been played here in this stadium for over two thousand years!"

DORIC

IONIC

CORINTHIAN

"Doric," Evi explained. "The beautiful posts holding up the roof. The Greeks are famous for the columns they built."

Athens was awesome!

But there was still
one thing left on
KeeKee's list…

"Oh...wait a minute," said KeeKee. "Plato was a *person!*"

"Yes," said Evi. "He was one of the smartest people ever."

"The great Plato was often found here, writing his books and teaching," said Evi.

"Plato wrote about a mysterious city called Atlantis," Evi said. "It is believed to be the sunken part of our Greek island, Santorini."

"There's Santorini!" said Evi.

"Long ago, its volcano erupted and
the middle of the island sank into the sea.
Some say that's the Lost City of Atlantis."

KeeKee noticed that all the buildings were blue and white. "Just like the Greek flag!" she exclaimed.

KeeKee and Evi had
so much fun on Santorini.

...rode a donkey...

They shopped for toys...

...ate fresh coconut...

...went for a swim...

...and took LOTS of pictures.

They ended the day
at the perfect spot.

"For you, KeeKee!" said Evi.
"A good-luck charm from Greece!"

"This has been the *best* day!"
said KeeKee.

Efcharistó.

Pronunciation Guide & Glossary

Words & Phrases

Antío.....................(a-DEE-oh).................................Goodbye

Efcharistó.............(ef-kha-ree-STOH)...............................Thank you

Kaliméra..............(ka-lee-MEH-ra)...........................Good morning

Kalí órexi..............(ka-LEE OH-reh-ksee)..............Enjoy your meal

Kalós orísate.......(ka-LOHS oh-REE-sah-te)....................Welcome

Kaló taksídi..........(ka-loh tak-SEE-dee).................Have a good trip

Moussaká.............(moo-sah-KA).........Meat & eggplant casserole

Niáou...................(nee-A-ow)..................................... Meow

Ópa......................(OH-pa).............................Greek exclamation

Oréo.....................(oh-REH-oh)................................ Beautiful

Parakaló..............(pa-ra-ka-LOH)........ You are welcome / Please

Taverna................(ta-VAIR-na)...........................Small restaurant

Tzatzíki................(tza-TZEE-kee)..............Yogurt & cucumber dip

Yiá sas..................(YA sas)...................Hello / Goodbye

Places

Parthenon – This temple was built 2,500 years ago and is one of the most famous buildings from Ancient Greece. It was dedicated to the goddess Athena, which is how Athens got its name.

Acropolis – The Parthenon is located on top of this huge hill in the center of Athens. "Acropolis" means "high city."

Places

Odeon of Herodes Atticus – Ancient amphitheater - a semicircle outdoor theater - built in 161 AD. Performances are still held here. "Odeon" means "theater."

Plaka – The oldest neighborhood in Athens. Its narrow, winding streets are still full of houses, ancient monuments, shops, and tavernas.

Panathenaic Stadium – Ancient Olympic stadium built in 556 AD. Also known as Kallimarmaro, which means "beautifully marbled" - it is built entirely out of marble.

Agora – The heart of ancient Athens, this area was the city's main market and meeting place. Democracy was invented here. The Agora is now a fascinating archaeological site. "Agora" means "gathering place."

Stoa of Attalos – A stoa (stoh-AH) is a covered walkway. Located in the Agora, this was the first-ever shopping mall. It has 45 Doric columns on the ground floor.

Santorini – Greece has thousands of islands, and this is one of the most famous. Its crescent shape is the result of a volcanic eruption thousands of years ago that blew out the center of the island. Ka-BOOM! It's home to Greece's last active volcano.